FUNNY FIRSTS™

CAMP ROTTEN TIME

by Mike Thaler • pictures by Jared Lee

Troll Associates

**For
cousin Brucie,
a friend indeed!**

M.T.

**For my mom
who didn't make
me go to Camp
Whatsmacallit.**

J.L.

Library of Congress Cataloging-in-Publication Data

Thaler, Mike, (date)
    Camp Rotten Time / by Mike Thaler; pictures by Jared Lee.
        p.   cm.—(Funny Firsts)
    Summary: Fearful of going off to camp, a child finds some comfort
when his seatmate on the bus expresses the same fears and they
decide to face them together.
    ISBN 0-8167-3024-5 (lib. bdg.) ISBN 0-8167-3025-3 (pbk.)
    [1. Camps—Fiction.] I. Lee, Jared D., ill. II. Title.
III. Series.
PZ7.T3Cam   1994
[E]—dc20   93-3231

FUNNY FIRSTS™ © 1994 Mike Thaler and Jared Lee
Text copyright © 1994 Mike Thaler
Illustrations copyright © 1994 Jared D. Lee Studio Inc.
Published by Troll Associates.

Printed in the United States of America.

10 9 8 7 6 5 4 3

I'm being sent to camp.

My mom and dad say it will be lots of fun.
I know it will be horrible!

Look at the list of things you need.
A canteen— for when you're lost
in the desert.

A pocketknife—
for when you're attacked by bears.

A flashlight—
for when you fall into a dark pit.

And you have to put your name
on *all* your clothes.
That's so they can identify the body.

I've never been away from home.
Why don't Mom and Dad go,
and I'll stay here?
They loved all the pictures
in the brochure.

The big lake—
in which I'll drown.

The big forest—
in which I'll get lost.

And the big mountain—
off which I'll fall!

And then there's the wildlife.
Big snakes that can eat you.

Big bears that can crush you.

Big squirrels that can grab
all your trail mix.

And the little wildlife.
Mosquitoes that can drink your blood
and give you incurable diseases.

Ants that crawl into your ears
and eat your brain.

And spiders that make big webs
to catch campers.

And if you survive the wildlife, there are activities. Hiking—I get tired crossing the street.

Canoeing — I don't feel safe
in the bathtub.

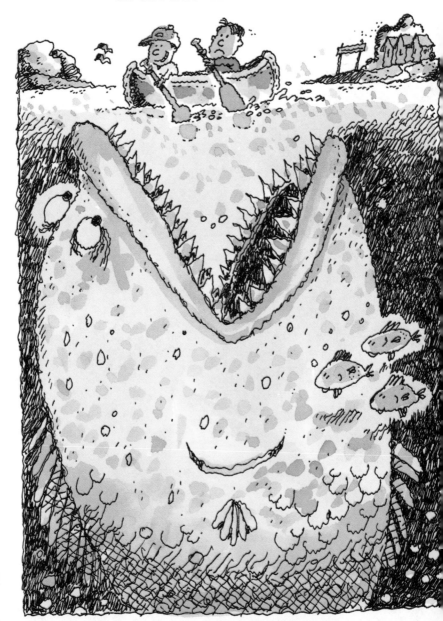

Kickball — big strangers will hurt me.

And if that doesn't finish you, there's the food! They don't call it the *mess* hall for nothing.

And if I get scared at night,
my mom won't be there.
No one will be there!
All I'll have is a flashlight.

Well, they've loaded my duffle bag.
They're leading me out the door.

We're in the car.

They're putting me on the bus.

I get on and sit down.

A big kid sits next to me.
He's got big muscles,
and tears in his eyes.
"My mom and dad are sending
me away," he sniffles.

"I'll fall into a dark pit."
"Don't worry." I smile.
"I've got a flashlight."

"I've got one, too!"
"That's super, we can
send signals at night."
"I know Morse code," he says, drying his eyes.

"And make funny hand shadows.
I know how to make a bear."

"And hold them under our chins to look spooky."
"I know lots of ghost stories."

"Gee, camp is going to be great!"
"Yeah!"